TWO HIKERS

REFLECTIONS AND STORIES FROM LIFE'S TRAVELS

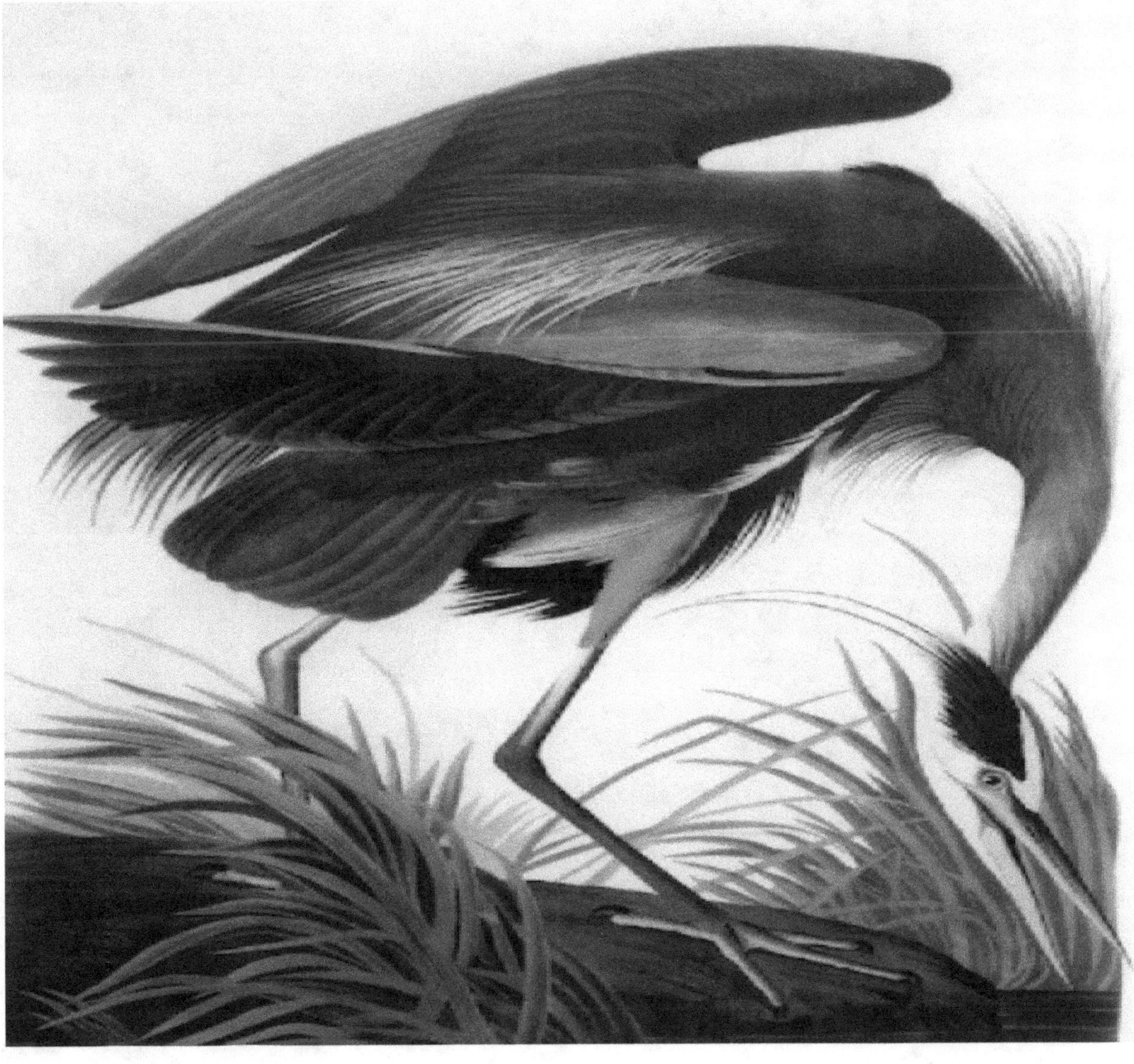

COLLECTION 1, WATERS

WINTER, 2026

Acadia National Park Waterfall Trail. Painting by Kate Keelen

Contents

Tucson Enchanted Hills Trails

Published By Two Hikers Press, Tucson, AZ

Co-Editors

Jerry Keelen

Nancy Jewett

Copies available on Amazon.com or full color PDF from TwoHikersAZ@gmail.com

Cover: John James Audubon, Birds of America, Great Blue Heron, Havell Ed. Plate #211

INTRODUCTION

TWO HIKERS

COLLECTION #1

Short Stories, Poems, Pics and More

A trail walked alone is always the same,

A trail walked by two is always different.

The main writers and co-editors of this first volume of Two Hikers magazine are winter time regular hikers in Tucson Mountain Park and many other Arizona trails.

Hiking the beautiful Sonoran Desert inspired in us an overflow of observations, viewpoints, memories and ideas. All of which are looked at and questioned from the perspectives of long and different life experiences. Our first collaboration was co-founding the Park West Writers Group and co-editing Volume One of the Park West Writers Magazine in 2023.

Whether in Tucson or away we trade drafts of our stories and essays, along with other writings about topics of personal interest for response, comment and critical review. Over time the correspondence has grown in volume and variety and some of it seemed like good enough writing (at least in our opinion) to share. We hope you agree!

We plan to solicit writings from other authors for future volumes of Two Hikers.

Nancy

Jerry

Mt. Tilacote, Tucson Mountain Park

Part One

Ferries and Waterborne Adventure

Ferry Kulshan

Author's note: This story was prompted by Edna St. Vincent Millay's poem of the same name.

RECUERDO

By Nancy Jewett

I remember sitting alone in the cabin of the Kulshan marveling at that unique moment. In the early 1970's, the Kulshan was the smallest ferry in the fleet of boats serving the islands of Puget Sound, part of the state's highway system. Ours was one of the shorter runs to a thinly populated island. It was the last run on a weekday after midnight. I parked on the open deck, the only car, and didn't even lock it. Why would I? I scrunched my shoulders and tucked my chin against the damp and cold temperature mixed by the dense salt laden breeze and the wind generated as the boat nosed away from the dock and into the night. I opened the heavy metal door that kept the cabin weather-tight and climbed the steps to the small narrow dimly lit waiting room. Two benches facing one another the length of the cabin. The walls holding safety notices. Unchanged from what it had been a multitude of times before. I was the only rider in the passenger cabin - maximum capacity -not many. Although I was safe inside the cabin, there was small relief from the dark and damp of my temperate marine world.

Describing rain was hard because it took so many forms that a single word wouldn't suffice - drizzle, mist, fog, low ceiling, heavy dripping from condensation against the ferry's surfaces, slippery. No matter, once the heavy door closed, the relative warmth of that protected space started to suffuse but not dry my clothing. Midnight, horns signaling departure and the acceleration of the engine signaled the beginning of a predictable amount of time in isolated peace for me. Transit from Mukilteo to Clinton was less than a half hour. A gentle rocking and plowing motion surrounded me providing the security to close my eyes and drift in the cushioned sounds of water and deeply bass engines.

That night I was alone being carried through the dark into Island Time. Island Time was both a shared dream state of mind and the slowed reality of people doing business and living life at slack tide. The past several months living on the Island turned out to be time spent between celebrating having achieved my life's dream by finishing my education, getting a great job and by my quest for him. The man who would be my life partner. The fellow who would cherish me as I would him.

I knew with my whole being that living on the Island with him was my future. The man I loved, the job I loved, the Island I loved. But fate added the twist that the intensity of his feelings was not reciprocal. Not because he was a bad man. Just that fate hadn't aligned our lives. Perhaps that realization is what fixed that night on the ferry into my memory. All alone I had to face that the image of my future might not happen. I thought I wanted the same life I'd been raised in in post WWII America.

But that wasn't the life I was living. Women's Lib messages surrounded me in the 1970's and an artsy version of life among creative people modeled the life I was living. I literally lived in a cabin in the woods. I had a dog and a Volkswagen bus. But I wanted him, my romantic life partner as well. It didn't seem like too much to ask for, and at first that's what he seemed to want too. My life and my dreams were uncomplicated. My thoughts that night must have burrowed into my deepest memories while I sat alone on that ferry traveling in a misty cloud inside and out. How little distance lay between a dream and being so deep in thought that a memory is created, colored, even matted and framed.

I couldn't see the dark hulk of the Island and I couldn't hear the gulls calling over the thrum of the engines, I didn't measure time until I became aware of the sounds' changing as we approached the landing and they reverberated off the high banks of the Island. We slowed and let the dolphins (pilings) and then the wing walls guide us to the dock. A bump. Now I was truly on Island time, I made my way to my car to await the signal to disembark.

And that's it. My memory of why I had been on the mainland nor of what I had done that day or the next day are simply not there. Not retrievable; apparently not relevant. But why is this memory so vivid? No lesson learned. No clear turning point in my life. Perhaps it was a foreshadowing of the future or maybe it was just that perfect moment of safety and rest and the Kulshan ferrying me home. I have no idea. But clearly this short time of quiet reflection has become, for me, a lifetime memory.

RECUERDO

By Edna St. Vincent Millay 1892-1950

We were very tired, we were very merry—
We had gone back and forth all night on the ferry.
It was bare and bright, and smelled like a stable—
But we looked into a fire, we leaned across a table,
We lay on a hill-top underneath the moon;
And the whistles kept blowing, and the dawn came soon.

We were very tired, we were very merry—
We had gone back and forth all night on the ferry;
And you ate an apple, and I ate a pear,
From a dozen of each we had bought somewhere;
And the sky went wan, and the wind came cold,
And the sun rose dripping, a bucketful of gold.

We were very tired, we were very merry,
We had gone back and forth all night on the ferry.
We hailed "Good morrow, mother!" to a shawl-covered head,
And bought a morning paper, which neither of us read;
And she wept, "God bless you!" for the apples and pears,
And we gave her all our money but our subway fares.

THE DIVER

In that instant just before the upward rise of the ship's bow, her knees flexed and her arms reached skyward. Exactly at the apex of the rise her knees dug deeper until with a sudden upward propulsion she launched herself from the railing. Coursing a perfect arc above the dark green water, her body positioned to pierce the surface at such a precisely vertical angle that on landing it was if the sea were sucking her in for its own. JK

. . . .

Seastreak highspeed ferry sails between Manhattan and Highlands, N.J.

TITAN OF THE TAFFRAIL

By Jerry Keelen

V. George Myers, had another lucrative day trading on Wall Street. As usual Vance, as he called himself to his wealthy New York metro clients, or George to those of the Iowa farm belt variety, stomped up the gang plank of the high-speed commuter ferry that waited, slightly bobbing, on this warm spring day at the South Street Seaport dock on the East River. Meyers high fived the mate and headed for the open-air "taffrail deck" at the back of the ferry. He had been taking the 50-minute ferry ride to and from the Atlantic Highlands in New Jersey for about a year and had endeared himself to the crew with his constant generosity. Generosity that secured his special place on the taffrail, as he called it, or on cold or rainy days in a private inside booth. Generosity also persuaded the crew to overlook Meyer's usual habit of indulging in a bottle or two of red wine and, on outside days, big cigars. Generosity that helped the crew and Captain to disregard the occasional complaints by female passengers of lewd remarks and creepy entreaties.

The ferry's powerful horn blasted and echoed off the towers of lower Manhattan. Thrusters delicately propelled the big catamaran-style ship from the dock out to the swirling green-gray current of the river. The pull of the out-going tide and the south bound current caught the ferry and started it spinning until the diesel propulsion system swelled up in a great and quickly rising rumble to conquer nature's forces and send the ferry on course down the river between the glass towers of the financial district and the charming brick townhomes and greenery of Brooklyn Heights on its way toward the open harbor and the Statue of Liberty.

Meyers, the American flag beginning to flutter up on the ship's pole behind him, leaned back in a white over-sized deck chair that somehow seemed to exceed in size and comfort any of the other deck chairs, which were few in number and coveted by weary commuters. He put his Louis Vuitton travel bag beside him, slipped off his tie, unbuttoned his white linen Brioni shirt, pulled a long cigar and gold lighter from his Brooks Brothers suit pocket and lighted up. A family looked at Meyers and his bluish redolent cigar smoke filling the deck. "You can't be serious, dude," the father said. "It's medicinal. Doctor's orders. Don't worry once we get crankin' the smoke will all blow off board and you won't smell a thing." "Well, I'm smellin' it now,'" Dad said. "Come on kids, let's get away from this stink. I'm reportin' you to the captain." "Suit yourself," Meyer said under his breath, "This is expensive smoke, way out of your league. And if you ever get to my dear Captain, you might be surprised to see he's got a whole box of these babies up there at the helm."

The ferry, christened the *Courageous*, accelerated with a jump once past the tip of Manhattan, now cruising by Lady Liberty at 20 knots, leaving a long wake of churned white seawater. Meyer unzipped the Louis Vuitton bag and pulled out a wine glass and a bottle of Tignanello Tuscan red. "Been a good day at the office, time for a good wine," he said to himself.

The Verrazzano Bridge loomed ahead. That's when the *Courageous* would accelerate to its top cruising speed of 38 knots – the fastest moving ship in the New York harbor, throwing up a "rooster tail" and trailing waves six feet high. That's when the green and silver glass buildings of Manhattan recede and magically appear to sit not on land but on the blue waters of New York harbor.

George Meyers uncorked the Tignanello and shakily poured some almost to the rim of his wine glass. He took the cigar from his clenched teeth, black hair blown back by the wind, and lifted his glass to drink. It is hard to drink on a moving deck in a 40 mile per hour wind. Red wine splashed onto his dark blue Brooks Brothers suit and reddened his Brioni collar and shirt front. Meyers didn't care, well maybe he hoped the Brioni could be cleaned after all it was a $500 customed tailored shirt. Small matter to Meyers though, his driver (technically his mother's driver) took everything to the cleaners at the end of every day. Besides he was cultivating his image as a man with money to burn, a man to be reckoned with. He peered up at the upper deck cabin window to see if any pretty young women were viewing his titanic display of wealth. His habit was to raise his glass to and wave down ones he found attractive, a tactic that sometimes worked.

Much to Meyers' chagrin, it was not nubile women, but rather a man about his own age stumbling down the stairway from the upper cabin. The *Courageous* had entered the open waters of lower New York Harbor and was gently rising and falling with the swells of the Atlantic. The man made it to the rail about ten feet from Meyers. Meyers gave the intruder a hard look and then began looking around for a crew member to remove him from Meyers' unofficially designated comfort zone.

"Mind if I crash here," the man tried to yell over the drone of 7,274 diesel horsepower forcing sea water through four propulsion jets. "Those kids up there are driving me nuts. Been a long day I need some rest." With that the man lowered himself to a prone position on the deck.

Meyers eyes were enraged. He arose from his chair, walked with imbalance resulting from the wind, the swells and the deck vibration, and said imperiously "Buddy, you can't stay there. This is my space."

"Your space? It's a public ferry. How do you get to have private space.?"

"Easy pal. I pay for it. Occupancy limits are strictly enforced by the crew."

"Well screw yourself. I'm not movin'."

Meyers eyed the man's basic work clothes and his jacket that said "Star of the Sea, Highlands, NJ, Porgies and Fluke" and said, "Very curious, you don't look like the type who can afford a ticket on this ferry." Meyers point being that the ferry was the most expensive commuter option from Manhattan to New Jersey and ridership was for that reason was essentially limited to high roller commuters and splurging day trippers.

The man said "Not that it's your business, but I grew up on the harbor and worked with half the guys on the crew one time or other. I help set the ropes and pump out the toilets in the morning. Let's say they give me a deep discount."

"Maybe I'll report you to the owners, then. My family knows them. Sounds like you're a free loading crook."

"And what do you do, mister big shot?"

"Trade and sell stocks and bonds on Wall St."

" 'Nough said," said the man. "And you're callin' me the crook?"

"You take the ferry every day?"

"That's the plan. I've got a new job in the city."

"Doing what?"

"What do you care?"

"Might want to get you fired," Meyers said with a laugh.

"Okay you asked, I'll tell you. I have a position at Pinkham and Breyer, that's a law firm."

"I know it well. Very blue chip. Acquisitions and mergers. You go to Harvard or Yale?"

"You got me, none of the above, I work in the mail room, associate doc shredder."

"No kidding. I thought all paperwork was electronic these days."

"A lot is I think and somebody in IT probably cleans that up. But there are a bunch of old partners and some younger lawyers too who only want to read paper. They put the old drafts or whatever in a secure box and send them down to me to be shredded."

Meyers flashed a Chesshire Cat-like grin, and said, "You seem like a decent hard-working guy. Sorry I jumped all over you. Name is Meyers, George Meyers and you?"

"Bernie O'Hanlon, at your service."

"I've got some good wine here, Bernie. Just so there's no hard feelings you want to try some?"

"Don't mind if I do, George. Just let me hop upstairs and get a paper cup from the concession."

The *Courageous* sped by a barnacled red channel buoy on the right. Meyers stared at the tossing marker without actually seeing it. He was thinking about an idea, not quite a plan yet, that he could cultivate over the next few days with his new friend Bernie O'Hanlon.

At the dock in Atlantic Highlands Meyers shook hands with Bernie and promised to meet him tomorrow to share some more wine and talk.

A black SUV was waiting to take Meyers to the family estate in Rumson. George opened the rear door and slung in the Vuitton bag and his soiled suit jacket. Then he opened the front door and climbed in.

"Good day, Georgie?" Ozzie, the driver asked with a British Midlands accent that had faded into mostly American English during his 35 years of service to the Meyers family. Meyers nodded. The drive through estates of forest-like Middletown to the Meyers' Rumson estate off Ridge Road took about 15 minutes. Ozzie pushed the button on the SUV's sun visor to open the security gate. He drove slowly along the curving crushed stone drive that went around back of the late 19th century brick manor-style house to the much smaller but stately brick and limestone two-story carriage house where Meyers stayed.

Meyers' mother, Clarice, got the mansion in the divorce after the detectives caught her husband Vance McCallum Meyers in not one but a multitude of compromising affairs and assignations. Clarice had suspicions of her husband's infidelities for many years, but decide to wait to see how his fortunes faired in the oil fields out in Oklahoma where he spent most of his time and many years building an oil boom empire. Indeed, the elder Meyers had become fabulously rich. When Clarice filed for divorce, Vance McCallum Meyers actually seemed pleased to turn over the Rumson estate to her together with a generous financial settlement. He said the mansion was old and stodgy and Rumson was a bore compared to his wild living out west.

V. George Meyers, his son, had an inherited self-centeredness, but also a mean, arguably cruel streak that as a child and teen included torturing pets. When his dad left, he did not argue for custody or show any interest in George or in bringing George into his oil empire. Thereafter, George's cruelty expanded beyond pets and increased exponentially. Police and private advocates appeared at the mansion on several occasions investigating or making claims of physical harm, threats and mental abuse by girls and women from high school through university. There were even hints that George was a person of interest in some unresolved date rape cases and the suspicious death of a young woman that investigators were perplexed about classifying as a suicide or a homicide. The family lawyers, Clarice, and wealthy uncles, Gilbert and Boyd Meyers, successfully intervened in every case, sometimes making large cash payments, to make George's problems go away.

Clarice had had enough of George imitating has dad's bad behavior and worse in her home and after college set him up in the carriage house. George wanted his own glory and more, but was powerless to acquire any of that without his own money. His uncles Gil and Boyd suggested to Clarice that at 26 years of age George ought to be working someplace, if only to channel his mind away from his perverse ways. They suggested the local brokerage house where they invested millions and could make the ask to employ George as an entry level sales associate.

In fact, Bing Barnes, the manager of the local brokerage had made a few such accommodations, theorizing that even if the kid had no aptitude for finance or sales, at least his rich relatives would invest good money in the firm simply out of appreciation for the favor. George got the job and Uncles Gil and Boyd made good on their expected largess, buying and trading large sums through Geroge at the firm. But George, highly motivated by greed, and possessing a kind of sociopathic first impression charm and energy, turnout to be a credible sales rep in his own right.

George bragged to co-workers that he would make enough money to buy a grand home on the water in Rumson or Middletown. He wanted his estate to exceed the value of his mother's estate. He implied that he wanted to impress his distant dad. Meyers figured he needed to make about $12 million dollars to buy the property and another $5 million for interior design and landscaping and to staff it with gardeners, chefs and maids. He wasn't going to make that kind of money in the local office so he schmoozed his uncles and the corporate office higher ups to get transferred to the flagship trading office in Manhattan.

George's main competitor at the local Red Bank office was Bartholomew "Barty" Stillwell, a young man of similar background and connections. Rivals at every turn they even taunted each other about their alpha male prowess, or lack thereof. George calling Barty a loser because of his propensity for dating chippies from what he called the local lower classes and Barty calling George a strange dude noting that he could never manage a relationship for more than one date. "Something wrong with you, Georgie boy?" Barty would spit. Their exasperated manager warned them both repeatedly to back off. The problem, at least at local level, resolved itself when George was promoted to the Manhattan office. Barty, of course, was enraged, and George was not a gracious winner.

The next day the late afternoon sun was bathing the *Courageous's* taffrail in warm light when Meyers and Bernie boarded within minutes of each other. George assumed his regular place on the taffrail. Bernie O'Hanlon arrived soon after and greeted Meyers heartily. "Hi Bern,"

Meyers said in response. "Look I've got some business to tend to for a bit. You mind coming back in about 20 minutes when the boat's rockin' and rollin'. We'll uncork a good one."

"Sure George, want me to bring back some lovely ladies?"

"Definitely later. First, I want to talk with you privately about something."

The diesels shifted into max power as the ferry made way under the Verranzzo Bridge. Bernie appeared. In the secure sound vortex of wind, engines and water Meyers and Bernie huddled for several minutes. Meyers talked and Bernie nodded his head in agreement several times culminating in handshake and Meyers taking a small envelope from the Louis Vuitton bag and quickly handing it to O'Hanlon. After that, George opened a fresh bottle of a Sonoma cabernet and the two drank heartily.

A week passed, and O'Hanlon approached George as the ferry churned past the Romer Shoal light about 15 minutes from docking in New Jersey. From a large sleeve inside his Star of the Sea oil-cloth jacket he removed a manilla envelope about three inches thick and dropped it on the deck near Meyers' Vuitton bag. Meyers after some brief banter, gave O'Hanlon another small white envelope. O'Hanlon quickly left for the inside cabin.

Romer Shoals Light Station *Photo credit: John Fish*

That evening Meyers, back at the carriage house, opened the envelope. He half-gasped at what he saw. It was a draft stamped "final proof" prepared for a senior Pinkham and Breyer partner's sign off. He saw that a large midwestern cloud-computing corporation called Linkador was poised to acquire the controlling stock shares of its competitor Abalone. With fore knowledge of the acquisition someone could purchase the stock of Abalone and turn a very large and fast profit. Meyers immediately texted his Uncles Gil and Boyd with the news. Meyers thought his uncles would take full advantage of this information and would credit him with uncovering a savvy opportunity.

Indeed, soon thereafter there was an unexpected rally in Abalone stock increasing its value rising well beyond what analysts had been predicting.

After that success, envelopes again passed between O'Hanlon and Meyers. O'Hanlon seemed to be very good or lucky at finding documents with golden nuggets of information. Meyers even became so bold as to try to contact his dad in Oklahoma about sure-thing stock deals.

He felt invincible, like the financial titan he always believed he was. Time for some twisted fun, he reasoned, as he toasted a group of young women looking at him from the upper cabin. He waived them down and three of them, looking to be about 20 years old, descended the stairwell to the Titan's lair. "Welcome ladies. I'm on a hot streak. Let me pour you some $500 wine. Throw whatever's in those paper cups over the rail and I'll treat you to best wine you'll ever taste."

"Thanks, Mister. Is that a real Louis Vuitton bag?" "Qui mademoiselle, and I've got the complete set at home. By the way, it's been a while since I've gone on spending spree in Paris. Anyone interest in that?"

The ladies giggled at the thought, none said "yes" but none said "no" either.

"What are you, some kind of Wall Street billionaire?"

"You've heard of the "Wolf of Wall St?" I'm the real one."

"Oooh. How about that wine?"

"Step right this way."

The tall athletic looking brunette with the blood red lipstick did just that and leaned in so close to Meyers' face she smelt his acrid wine and cigar smoked breath.

"I like your lipstick," Meyers said as he poured wine into her lipstick impressed paper cup.

"You do? How sweet. Would you like little sample?"

Meyers was thinking pucker up, but the tall woman deftly hooked Meyers' elbow with hers and put her cup to Meyers lips and his wine glass to hers. They drank and she laughed and they drank again. "See," she said, "My lipstick is in on your glass." The other women stood back looking a bit coy in the face of the boldness of their friend.

After some small talk, Meyers tried to convince the tall one to let him take her out later that night. They exchanged phone numbers and he a leering lust twisted look and she a "come hither" look.

The ferry slowed as it neared the bulkhead by its dock. A crew member with a clear trash bag came around and collected the cups and other trash on the taffrail. He motioned for Meyers to trash the empty wine bottle, but Meyers defiantly tossed it, as was his habit, backwards over the rail. The Courageous docked and everybody filed off of into the cool soft evening air of the Highlands of the Jersey Shore.

SEC computers are programmed to detect irregular trading in moribund stocks, especially ones that might be announced as targets of a takeover and enhanced stock value. FBI agents skilled at investigating such suspicious computer blips soon discovered that the common denominator in some recent anomalies was the presence of Pinkham and Breyers, the law firm that represented either the buyer or seller in certain pending mergers and acquisitions.

FBI Special Agents reviewed the Pinkham and Breyer's document security practices and personnel background dossiers. They quickly identified document shredder Bernard O'Hanlon as a person of interest. They also looked to see who was purchasing the stocks. It fell together for them quickly, but they need one more piece of evidence. They need to see O'Hanlon deliver a package of insider information to someone.

The agents were notified by O'Hanlon's supervisor that his shredded materials weighed less that the documents given to him for shredding by about 18 ounces. Investigators shadowed him to the South Street Seaport docks that afternoon and boarded the *Courageous*, staking out positions throughout the craft ready to act if O'Hanlon made his drop.

The ferry was churning passed the Statue of Liberty when O'Hanlon made his move, a little sooner than before to avoid repeating a pattern.

"He's on the move," the agents radioed to their colleagues. "Heading for the stairs to the open deck. On the way down the stairs. Walking toward the gray-suit guy in the chair in front of the flag."

Three agents were in position to observe the transaction. O'Hanlon nodded to Meyers and tossed the envelope so that it leaned against the Louis Vuitton bag and slipped down flat on the deck. Meyers took a small white envelope from his suit jacket pocket and handed it to O'Hanlon. O'Hanlon turned to leave and three FBI agents stepped in front of him. The lead agent yelled, "Stop where you are. Hands on your head."

Meyers groaned, "it's over..." and put his hands half over his head and half over his eyes.

The lead agent said “Bernard O’Hanlon, you are under arrest for suspicion of insider trading, you have the right to remain silent, anything you say can and will be held against you....” and he went on with the Miranda Warning while O’Hanlon was cuffed and taken into custody by the agents.

Law enforcement was showing up in force on the pier and the ferry parking lot, red, white and blue flashers flashing in profusion. The blood had drained from Meyers face, his legs turned rubbery and he could no longer stand. His hands dropped from his face and he slumped into his oversized deck chair. “What about me?” Meyers managed to call out to one of the agents.

“What about you? You want to be arrested too?”

“No, no, that’s not what I meant. You mean you don’t care about me?”

“Sorry pal. Hope you’re not disappointed.”

“No,” he mouthed weakly.

Meyers left the boat and Ozzie drove him straight home. Clarice and Uncles Gil and Boyd were waiting.

"George. You look pale," said Uncle Gil.

"No problem. Fine, I had a little scare, if you mean by the way I look, might be catching a cold."

"We'll I hate to break it to you George, but all is not fine. The FBI came calling and asked if any of us got any stock tips from you. We all admitted that we did, but one way or another we all said the same thing - Georgie is a dim-wit and anyone taking advice from him is a double dim-wit. Your Dad said stuff about you that I won't repeat, because no dad should say things like that about his son. Sorry, Georgie."

"But Uncle Gil, if none of you bought any stocks, how did the prices get kited up? Somebody must have been buying."

"Yeah, I called Bing Barnes at your old office in Red Bank to see if he had any ideas. He said the SEC was in looking at Barty Stillwell's trading. Barty's been suspended and it doesn't look good for him. He said Stillwell is a guy you had a nasty falling out with.

"Looks like other people did buy for sure, but not based on anything you said. O'Hanlon was pals with Stillwell from way back. Barnes thinks Stillwell might have made some sales through dark off-shore accounts, or something along those lines. He used that O'Hanlon guy to set you up. He must have figured that the insider trading would be triggered by your tips to your relatives. I guess he figured he'd cover his tracks and you would take the fall. It didn't work because we didn't buy or spread your stupid trading tips around. We had no idea they came from insider trading stuff either. We didn't give you credit for that level of stupidity."

"Stillwell's none too bright either to think he could get away with it."

Meyers said, "He's a dirt bag. Everyone knows that. I hope he goes to jail and dies."

"Anyway George, no one acted on your advice so whether you're an inside trader or enabler is debatable according to our lawyer. He doubted that you will be charged."

"I feel great. Off the hook. Thanks Uncle Gil, you too Uncle Boyd."

"Not so fast, the County Prosecutor is waiting over at the carriage house."

"Why?

"Rape and murder. We've brought in a criminal lawyer to prevent you from saying anything stupid, incriminating I guess is the proper word. We've packed a bag for you. Hopefully, they'll let you take it to the county jail overnight. They say you will be held in an isolated cell to protect you from attacks. It seems that what your being charged with are the kinds of things that get jailhouse reprisals."

Meyers lost his color for the second time.

County prosecutor Santana, accompanied by a tall looking brunette with blood red lipstick, said as soon as George appeared, "Vance George Meyers, you are under arrest for the rapes of two women, I'll only identify them at this time as Jane Does, and manslaughter in the death of Laura Ditmas."

Meyers mouthed "you" as he stared at the tall brunette wearing the FBI vest. Then he was taken to prison.

At the press conference that followed Santana praised the cooperation of law enforcement in the investigation. He noted that the missing evidence, Meyers' DNA sample, was obtained by creative but lawful means on a paper cup collected by agents on the ferry *Courageous* out of Highlands, New Jersey.

The next morning the ferry sped as usual to Manhattan, but the Titan was absent. The crew read the account of fall of V. George Meyers and said they never liked him anyway.

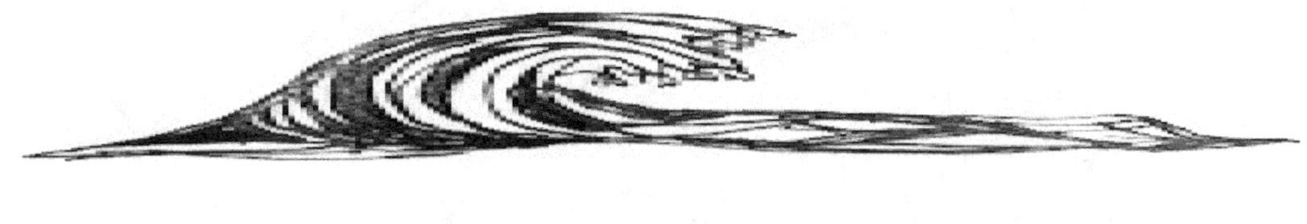

....

BEYOND THE BLUE MIST

By Nancy Jewett

The three of us carried the last of our packs and foodstuffs onto the dock. It had been a long but beautiful trip along the Sunshine Coast of British Columbia. We had driven our '71 Datsun pickup through customs at Blaine, Washington along the coast road to Lund, British Columbia where we were to meet Ron and his boat. Using self-discipline and self-promotion, Ron had become an authority on petroglyphs and pictographs of the Northwest Coast. He had convinced the Provincial government to give us permission and funds to document several sites along the Inside Passage. We had camera, rubbing materials, muslin, heel ball and a well-stocked art box. My husband, Mike, was a talented archaeology student. Our anticipation erased any apprehension I may have felt about three weeks on board a 30-foot handmade trimaran with a nine-horse outboard to supplement our sails.

Bear Claw Totem

As I carried my pack from the dock down two steps into the galley I was stopped by my doubts. Our boat had all the comforts of home - in very tight quarters. The galley was split by the single passage way that extended to the 'v' berth in the bow. On my right, as I ducked into the cabin, was the wood fueled heating and cooking stove mounted waist high as was most of cabin's furnishings. The cabin hung over and was supported by the struts reaching from the slender main hull attaching to each of the lateral hulls. It was narrow for our feet but quite roomy above our knees. On the left of the companionway was the galley sink. Settees lined either side with a long narrow table built in on the left. All our gear and food was secured deeply into the wings of the cabin. The wings gave us ample head and arm room and a sense of spaciousness visually if not actually. There were small portholes along eye level just below the ceiling that provided light. Functional would describe the color and style of the lounge. There was no 'boat chic' here.

To the right just before the entrance into fore or 'v' berth or sleeping cabin was the head. Try to visualize the entire lounge or living space, each side of the main cabin hung out over the sea suspended on the struts that were each connected to a pontoon, one on each side. A trimaran - a three hulled boat. On one of the upper shelves above the settees was a round hole and a lid had been cut out to allow for a seat. All I had to do was climb from the narrow walking passage onto the lounge bench, turn around as I was doffing my trousers and sit on the hole. It did require leaning forward as the ceiling and the end wall of the main cabin formed a tight low corner here. A privacy curtain had not been deemed necessary.

I stood in the galley that first time aboard, while my eyes adjusted to the dimness, the overwhelming and lasting impression was the smell. Our boat didn't have any refrigeration. All our food was canned, preserved or dried. Rings of dried smoked sausages were strung on ropes and hung all along the long walls of our main cabin. Herbs, garlic, a smoky tang met with the soft slapping of the water on our hull which caused the sausages to swing gently creating a constant essence of movement in the musky dimness. My stomach roiled.

The rocking of the boat, my motion sickness and my anticipation all settled into resonance which became my sea legs. Ron gave us a few pointers about living aboard and we each found our 'places' both above and below deck. Ron stood just outside the cabin door where he could operate the rudder, watch the wind telltale, and see the water and the shore. Mike and I liked a variety of spots on the cabin roof. As we moved away from Lund we truly moved into a world Beyond the Blue Mist.

This world exists in a timeless mixture of First Nation villages moldering on forgotten islands swallowed in blackberry vines, bees and mellowing sunshine that moves slowly through the trees. It's the same timeless mist that shrouds all of the variety of human habitation along this fractured continental edge. Among these islands we encountered a clapboard home built on a floating log raft, the current inhabitants gracious and anxious for conversation, tea and news. Nearby the imagined sounds of Asian languages floated on the mists coming from the abandoned cannery dormitories. This mist also filled the little bay where the orca played tag with us unaware of the rules of contact. We were Beyond the Blue Mist indeed.

Our mission was to document petroglyphs, pictures pecked into rock by First Nation people, for reasons we have yet to clearly understand. One of the most dramatic images we documented was that of the 1788 Meares sailing ship we found many feet above the water.

These places of mist and hanging moss, warm speckles of sunlight and the chill of the dense canopy absorbed even the ambient sound of our current existence. Bellingham and Olympia were no more real than Village Island or Blind Passage.

18th Century Petroglyph Sailing Ship (photo credit unknown)

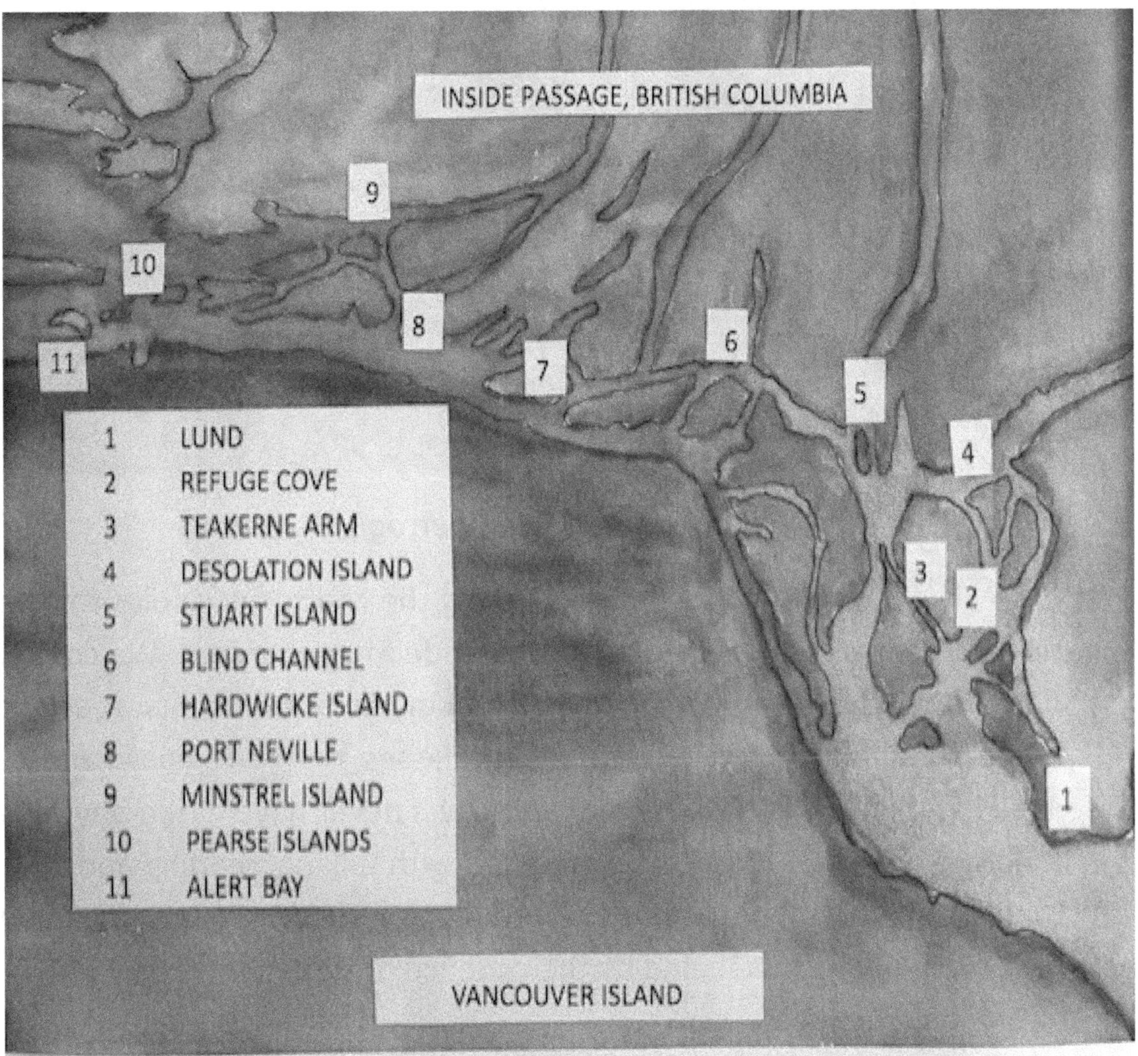

Our exploration from Lund, British Columbia to Alert Bay

One night we docked at Bones Bay, the site of an abandoned cannery. The cannery manager's old home was presently being inhabited by a young fisherman and his family. The cannery, a huge gaping building, was sliding askew down a slope pressed by its own weight. It had created one of those 'fun house' structures where gravity and the horizontal were optically opposed. Next door we found the dormitory filled with 4 X4 foot by 6-foot cubicles for workers.

Neville Island Deer, petroglyph rubbing

The days turned to weeks checking the charts and tables for the best tides to gain access to the islands we needed to document. We cooked daily innovative treats using sausage and my favorite- Sailors' toast. It was twice baked, full of whole grains and molasses, then dried hard and kept in in air-tight jars. Mildly sweet and crunchy, I never have eaten anything like it before or since. Our nights were filled with talking, reading and meditation but not of the popularized Eastern mode. Ours was of quiet drifting thoughts marshaled by the cadence of slap-on-hull.

It was beautiful out in the islands. Morning mists, gentle sufficient breeze to sail on and sun. Sunlight that was sometimes weak and moistened by the mist or the actual breath released by the forest-CO_2 in and O_2 out, CO_2 in and O_2 out. Sometimes the sun blazed creating a desire to sunbathe, hike to the high hill or just nap. I felt in awe again of the vagaries of Nature. How in the world could we be this far north and still enjoy these temperate days? The Japanese current raced past this part of Canada and filled the Inside Passage during the floodtides. Then for hours and hours each day as the tide ebbed the tepid water slowly released its warmth among the small rocky islands.

And then it disappeared. That reassuring sunshine was gone like a good mood or a happy conversation. It was masked and distorted by a storm. Dark clouds chilled the air. Menacing rocky shores replaced moss softened stepping stones. Everything became treacherous. Our decks were slippery. Our moorage was fragile in the lee of a little unnamed island on the western edge of Johnstone Straits. Coolness and moisture seeped into the cabin. The hatches had to be resealed. Stove wood kept dry. Wet clothes hung from the same ropes that had held our diminishing supply of sausages. We had to get to Alert Bay and the east side of Vancouver Island. Our documenting task was completed. Our food and fuel supplies were low and our spot on the return ferry in jeopardy.

But the seas were dangerously high – wind against tide gave angry rough seas. Wind blowing with the tide gave great standing waves and troughs. At 4 AM of the second storm day Ron decided the wind and water looked navigable. We pulled the little anchor, coiled the mooring lines and carefully nosed out into the current. Despite the sounds, spray and literal bucking of our craft we made steady progress. Ron at the rudder and Mike on deck managed the sails at Ron's command. I stayed out of the way with my head out of the hatch enough to watch our progress. Besides, the blast of air into my face helped my nausea in contrast to the closeness of the cabin.

We had finally left the marginal protection of the islands to cross open water to Alert Bay. I was terrified. The spray and wind and heave and smack of our boat were more that my balance and orientation organs –

stomach and inner ear and feet- could take. I went to the berth to try to lie down but to my dismay I was startled by sea water coming in the hatch at an alarming rate. I yelled to Ron. He said our bilge pumps were working and would try to keep up. I decided if I was going to die I would be warm so I put on all of my clothes. Finally, frightened and bumping my way back to the cabin hatch I stuck my head out to watch once more. Our main sail was carrying us with the wind across the straits making steady progress.

Suddenly the brass snap shackle failed! Our mainsail fluttered and flopped. Ron called to Mike to catch it - this powerful curtain, flopping wildly free of the boom. Mike set about on all fours across the roof of the cabin to the mast and after stabilizing the boom attempted to drop the mainsail - lines, yards of cloth, water and wind, despite the constant pounding of the hulls. No one spoke, No one breathed. Finally, he got it down tangled lines and all. Meanwhile Ron had started the nine-horse and

whenever it could reach the water at the bottom of a trough and during the upslope of a swell we would progress. Then as we topped the swell it would whine in the air until it grabbed water again down slope. Bottom of a trough and up again over and over. Green walls of water all around us.

Apparently, the Harbor Master of Alert Bay saw us coming. As we approached, we were able to get some protection from the land mass. We limped into the gas dock where they were waiting for us. Normally you cannot tie up for longer than you need to gas up but exceptions are made. Several men secured our boat and assisted us. My land legs were loath to return to me because of my tremors. I began to understand what we had risked and succeeded to preserve. Mike helped Ron pump the bilge and refuel. I tried to straighten up the cabin from all the tossing and banging. They also began some of the simpler repairs before we made our way to the visitors dock and rafted up alongside several others sitting out the storm.

Yellow legs (the Canadian Mounted Police) checked our passports to be sure they were in order. And we were checked out by our peers. Well maybe we were pure fools! Or were we competent, innovative, lucky sailors? Ultimately, we were all of those. Some of the old salts dismissed us out of hand. Everyone was kind but some were as kind as a Protestant Sunday school teacher would be. Some few were complimentary of our skills that kept us seaworthy. A few granted that good luck was for fools and Americans!

I accepted the fact that we had been protected by good spirits and talented captaining. We had been respectful at the burial island. We had left our moorages unsoiled and we had brought companionship and conversation to the residents Beyond the Blue Mist.

Orca, Credit Detroit Institute of the Arts

Part Two

Spirt Guides: *Heron-ymus* and *Wave and Albatross*

HERON-YMUS

By Nancy Jewett

When she was 12, she read a book called *Karen* by Marie Killilea. It was about a young girl who had been born with cerebral palsy, but to her 12-year-old self, it was a book about the secondary character, the physical therapist. The therapist who taught Karen, the main character, the skills she needed to be able to move through life. When the girl finished reading the book she thought, "that's what I want to do."

As it turned out, she didn't like being around other children. She liked being in her room reading. She was fit and strong and capable, but she much preferred one or two friends, a good book, sitting outside in the trees or cozy in her home. She wasn't an athlete and didn't like competitive sports or even individual sports for that matter.

She was a good student; a diligent student so High School had been easy for her, but at the University she had to work very hard to achieve B's in her classes. When she first applied to the School of Medicine, Physical Rehabilitation, Physical Therapy program which selected 20 students out of applicants from five states, she made the cut as first alternate and that year no one dropped. That was a crushing blow but taught her solidarity of purpose and determination. The next year she tried again, studied hard, and learned how to sell herself. She learned how to make eye contact and smile and speak up and be clear about why she wanted to be a Physical Therapist, PT. When she met her PT classmates, many were still or had been athletes. That's why they knew about PT. Not by reading a young adult book or by volunteering.

During those three prerequisite years waiting to get accepted into the Medical School PT program, she met her requirement of volunteering. This requirement was in place to assure the selection committee that an applicant actually knew what she was getting into. By volunteering she knew what her role in the world would be and it also allowed pre-PT students to find their niche, geriatrics or orthopedics or pediatrics.

During those three prerequisite years at the end of her teens she volunteered at a VA hospital at the height of the Vietnam War. She volunteered to assist young men who were her age. She witnessed the horrific effects of booby traps and Napalm. Those young men taught her how essential mobility was to their lives. As basic as to roll over in bed on their own, to get out of the bed on their own, to operate a wheelchair or crutches, all meant independence. In their minds, independence meant increased amounts of dignity. She wanted to be part of that.

For her, the most basic attraction to PT, was to find ways to help people acquire the skills to enable them to achieve the movement they wanted possess or activity to pursue. But another reason she felt strongly was the beauty of all movement; its fluidity and efficiency, the marvel of the mechanics of movement and balance. She loved dance and admired gymnasts. She loved to ski.

University of Washington

During her classes she studied the mechanics and physics of nature. She was awed by the wind in the trees, the interplay of loads and levers and of hydraulics. She watched trees swing in the breeze and waves coming to shore. The mastery and mystery of the laws of nature built her belief in something greater than mankind. She developed her philosophies of living in the natural world and in the redemptive personal power of people. People whose suffering was alleviated by learning to harness as much of nature's mechanics and physics as they could to their advantage.

To her the birds were like dancers. They took their power and strength of mobility and added gracefulness and efficiency and endurance. Her focus upon the birds came in her mid-20s when she was living very close to the world of the Northwest Coast Native Americans. Their ideas of totems and spirits and their stories of the powers that Raven or Eagle or Heron carried had been told for millennia. Thinking about the enduring truths of those stories caused her to wonder about a totem that she could identify with. She knew it was the Great Blue Heron. She aspired to its

Great blue heron *Photo credit: Paul Brennan*

elegance, its efficiency; its confidence was admirable; it's stoicism. Its power lifting itself into flight modeled grace under pressure. She noted its very diet. It's willingness to take what was available. It's delicacy. It's wonderful gait.

The most wonderful things happened when the heron became a part of her. When her life met difficult times and difficult challenges, uncertainty, or a loss of confidence, she would look out along the road side or while walking the beach and there would be a heron, a Great Blue Heron, just the sight of which immediately reminded her that she possessed the tools she needed, the resources she could rely on; that her power when applied gracefully could sustain her or extricate her from the world when it became too much. The Great Blue Heron became the obvious symbol when it was important for personal reasons for her to have a totem tattoo. She carries a Great Blue Heron with her as an emblem and a reminder of her spirit guide for the rest of her days.

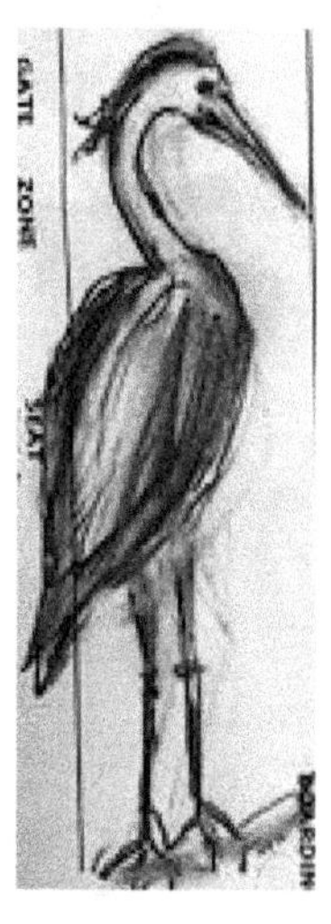

WAVES AND ALBATROSS

By Jerry Keelen

My friend and fellow hiker mentioned in passing that she has a spirit totem or guide that helps her be alive to the core nature of her being. A spirit guide, she explained, is usually an animal that exhibits traits such as patience, stealth and strength that a person might also share or aspire to. She learned about spirit guides from being interested in Native American practices and culture, especially, having grown up in Washington State, among the tribes of the Pacific Northwest. Being an easterner the idea of adopting a spirit animal had never occurred to me. In New Jersey contact with Native American culture is usually limited to going to a casino. It sounded like a quaint harmless idea. After talking with my friend, I was surprised to learn of the depth of her belief and commitment to her totem. She told me that for 30 years she has had a beautiful tattoo of her spirit guide, but she made me guess what it was.

My first guess was "99 out of 100%" wrong, she said. A little desperate not to commit further insult, I began studying the internet for the attributes of typical spirit guide animals. My friend did not seem to be much akin to a bear, fox, wolf, eagle, fish, seal or anything else, and my first guess "owl" was already ruled out. Finally, probably sensing my discomfort, she relented and told me her spirit animal is the Great blue heron. And for good reason. Like her, the Great blue is elegant, intelligent, patient, deliberate, accurate, skilled and adaptable in the ways of survival.

After learning all this I thought that I might adopt a spirit animal and also a nature totem which I learned is another practice in many native cultures. Exactly why I thought that I couldn't say, but clearly my friend found her guide useful when she needed clarity and that seemed like a worthy enough reason for me too. Being raised Catholic, I sometimes think about my namesake St. Jerome and everybody's favorite, St. Francis, as examples when I try to write clearly (Jerome was a famous writer) or to remember to be a more charitable person like Francis. The general concept of seeking spiritual guidance is therefore, for me, a familiar concept.

To my surprised I discovered that I already had what were in effect my nature totem and a spirit animal, I'd just never thought of them that way.

Waves

One of the first joys and mysteries of my life were ocean waves. Well before I could swim, my father would take me in his arms and wade into the ocean. On special days at high tide the waves would peak close to the shore and carry us up, it seemed like, to the sky, and then let us down gently as they continued their travels to the beach. My father would go "Whooo, up we go" and I'd go "Whooo" with him. The waves would come in sets and we could see them forming green humps maybe 200 yards out. Occasionally, a very big wave would come in with a set of regular ones and Dad would say “hold tight, I won’t let you go”, and I’d grip his neck with all my might. If a wave was very big it would sometimes crest before reaching shore and we’d get overtopped by the green curl and whitecap churn of the about to fully break wave. My dad and I would be underwater for a moment and then resurface. I did not find that part fun at all. In fact, the idea of a dunking terrified me and coughing salt water out of my mouth and nose, my eyes blurry, I’d yell “I want to get out.” Dad would say that that was part of the fun, but I wasn’t buying it. He would then take me back to the beach and I’d play in the sand and look at my big sister and cousins being lifted high and fully engulfed inside the translucent sunlit Coke-bottle green waves like angels suspended between earth and heaven. My fear never lasted more than ten minutes and back I’d go gripping Dad and loving every second.

I’m not sure when, but sometime in early adolescence I began to sit on the beach and look at waves and wonder what they really were. The water was going up and down, but not visibly progressing forward. At least it did not appear to be moving forward, only some mysterious energy that eventually reached shore with a crashing foamy rush onto the beach. Wind would affect the waves. A wind from the east would drive in big rollers. A west wind would flatten the ocean surface, except on perfect days when powerful big waves coming from a faraway major Atlantic depression came storming in and were met by a strong wind coming directly off the shore. The result was perfectly formed giant waves with wind whipped diaphanous contrails of spray flying back from their tops. These were big fast predictable waves that as I grew into my later teen years would draw surfers from near and far.

Wave energy I learned was generated by atmospheric wind energy being transferred to the water surface. I also learned that that energy would pass through the water until friction or a beach or cliff wall would dissipate it. If energy raises the crest of a water wave between the fore and aft troughs by a ratio of 1 over 7 the wave will break from the top and fall forward.

I learned the how of waves, but still the idea of watching an unseeable moving force in action was mystical. There is hardly anything like it, and to me a well-formed wave is the most perfect shape in nature.

"Catch a wave and you're sitting on top of the world," the Beach Boys harmonized. And that became a truism and an anthem for me. I started surfing in the "big board" era which was at the being of the fast-growing sport in the 60s. I felt like I was in motion with and part of nature's thrilling show of power.

The Atlantic is often choppy and difficult to surf. But my favorite time of the year was September when the crowds were gone, the water warm, clear, calm and often the waves where well-formed rollers rising about a hundred yards off shore.

My board, a Dewey Weber Performer, was about 10 feet long and was big enough to walk around on. "Hang Ten" was a popular phrase back then. It meant that a surfer could walk to the nose of the board, counter-balanced by the weight of the water on the tail end of the board, and literally stand with ten toes over the front of the board. The Weber Performer was the perfect board to execute that feat. September was the perfect time to do it. I loved standing tall on the board and watching the sand rills, calico crabs and sometimes fish and even once a sea turtle passing below my board.

Hanging Ten on a Weber Performer, Photo credit: Dewey Weber Surfboards

I surfed long enough to be part of the evolution to the “short board” which basically is a small light board that is a good vehicle to carve up and down wave surfaces and do tricks like 360s. The short board now predominates and most surfing competitions are scored based on the surf-rider’s short board agility. I traded in my big board for a Dusty Rhodes Love which is about half the size of the Performer. But I always preferred the grace and oneness with the wave of my long board. The short board to me seems to put the focus on the surfer and in a way dishonors the dignity of the wave. People have a way of turning every beautiful natural thing into a competition from surfing, to bird watching, to river kayaking and beyond.

I still love to watch waves at the beach and I know I always will. There is beauty, but the underlying force of energy pulsing through the water is what excites me. We are told that babies are over 75% water and adults are on average between 55% and 60% water. I think that waves pulse inside of me, causing movement, joy and well-being. Waves, I now appreciate, are my nature totem and have been from the beginning.

Albatross

My spirit animal or guide, like the waves and my friend's Great blue heron, is one of long standing. Before I proceed, I must admit that I have never seen my spirit guide, the Laysan Albatross, even though there are thought to be over a million of them flying around the Northern Pacific. I became an avid birdwatcher in my mid-20s, walking the Jersey Shore beaches and noticing that there were many different kinds of shore birds. My first "look up" bird was a black-bellied plover picking over the tideline for tiny bits of food. The black-bellied plover is big, but even I could tell, was clearly not a seagull.

After that my fascination with identifying birds grew quickly. I got two field guides, binoculars and took a mail order course from the Cornell Laboratory of Ornithology. The are over 7,000 bird species worldwide of all sizes and survival strategies from tinniest hummingbirds to the massive Condors of California and the Andes.

I think what first drew me to the albatross was imagining myself extending and stiffening new found long, rigid, narrow wings and being alive to updrafts and wind shears projecting off undulating blue Pacific waves. Sensing the slightest pressure changes and barely moving my long wings, I'd feel one with the wind and sea. I'd watch for the mountainous shores of Japan and Hawaii, and rocks and sands of the Aleutian Islands and California. I'd see the sunrise and sunset over the vastness of the Pacific and never get tired.

Japan's Mt. Fuji

I also share the Laysan's preference for warmish water. Unlike many Antarctic albatross cousins born to thrive in harsh and frigid regions of the South Seas, Laysans breed in the relative comfort of atolls of the northern Hawaiian Island chain.

Scientists have banded them there for generations. They live at least 75 years and even older ones remain fertile and capable of raising a new chick to adulthood every year. Laysan albatross are solitary except during mating season and while raising their chicks, at which time they are sociable and generally when back on land are paired-off for life.

Albatross often cover tens of thousands of ocean miles without touching land. Their wings are designed to catch the chaotic wind shears and updrafts off massive Pacific waves. They glide, or wind surf, in a figure 8 pattern without wasting energy by flapping. Normally they will fly between five and 60 feet above the water. Albatross have evolved interesting survival mechanisms, including sleeping in flight with half their brain dozing while the other remains alert, a phenomenon called "uni-hemispheric" sleep - all the while swooping down to the surface to scoop up squid, cuttle-fish, and small fish swimming in large schools. Also, they can drink ocean water and filter out the salty minerals through internal glands that extrude the salt through their beaks.

I like to think I share important characteristics with the Laysan Albatross. While I may not possess all of the skills and attributes of the bird, those that I don't are ones that I aspire to. I have been a long-distance runner since high school. In my late 60's a few years ago, I completed, run by run, a pieced together a circumnavigation of the planet. My kids gave me a sticker for the car that says,"24,901" miles, trumping all the 13.1, 26.2 and even 100K stickers commonly seen on cars. My miles were mostly logged alone over the course of many years. Since then, I've added probably another five thousand miles. My spirit animal, of course, far exceeds such distances, but in essence we are coursing an in-common, solitary path, beyond the reach of friends, foes and civilization.

We are not unsociable though. I enjoy running and hiking company when I can get it, it's just that there aren't a lot of people who want to run all the time. I enjoy being around people when I'm not running too. The Laysan birds I'm sure feel the call to be with their kind come breeding time when these sociable birds gather by the hundreds of thousands.

Albatross and I are tough, resourceful and adaptable by nature. I don't claim to drink sea water, or put half my brain to sleep the way nature has equipped the Laysan albatross to do. I do seem to need less sleep than most and I wear a hydration vest when covering longer distances or when temperatures rise.

I try to maneuver the metaphoric updrafts and wind shears of life well too.

Laysan albatross visit every corner of the Northern Pacific. I enjoy travel, but don't go on the road or sky to new places as much as I'd like. My spirit guide is a great example being among the greatest travelers on the planet.

Laysan's are fit and have a track record of being extraordinarily long-lived. Those things are only partially within my control, but certainly ones that I aspire to.

We, my spirit animal and I, have few enemies and live peacefully, neither attacking others nor being attacked.

Laysan albatross live wild and free. They have the courage to leave the atoll when it is time to fly away. I know I won't achieve that level of wildness or freedom, but at least I can be mindful of my spirit guide, always free in flight, and seize the day when opportunities arise.

In the beginning, I said that I am new to the spirit guide world, and while choosing mine has been easy I am left with a quandary. Do I need to get a tattoo? My spirit animal and nature totem are often paired. Perhaps a Laysan albatross flying over a wave would be the thing?

. . . .

Part Three

Formative Days: *Tattoo* and *Hot Dog Boy's Day*

TATTOO

By Nancy Jewett

It was about 4 o'clock in the afternoon and I was hanging out at the Nurse's Station having finished treating my patients for the second time that day. I was tired and ready to go home.

I looked down the hall and could see the nurses from the Emergency Room were rolling a gurney up the hallway toward us. It looked like there was about to be a new admission to the medical floor. When they arrived, the ER nurses asked if we could help transfer the new patient into their bed.

"It'll be a maximum assistance transfer needing five people, if possible, but three at the minimum," they suggested. We had four.

Being a physical therapist, I was the de facto leader of our spontaneous transfer team. I started assessing our patient. *She was very old and not alert or oriented. She'd had a stroke. Good, no fractures, but she'd be frail and a dead lift.*

I asked one nurse to take her head, one her feet, another and I would take her midsection because that is the heaviest part.

We had a transfer sheet, a sheet folded in half under the patient's bottom and trunk, to help 'sling' their weight across the gap between the gurney and the bed. If a patient was conscious, I'd explain what we were doing and how they could help. If not, I usually said something like,

"*Their name*, we are going to move you onto the bed on the count of three".

The nurses on the far side of the bed sometimes had to crawl up on the bed because sometimes the gurney could be raised or lowered enough to match the bed height and sometimes it couldn't. I had to make my assignments based upon the equipment we had and the height and strength of the staff available.

I took a quick glance again at the patient. She was not awake.
"One, two, three, go."

As they pulled and we lifted her hips, the top sheet pulled away and exposed her right hip to me. There was sweet hand-done tattoo of a heart, an arrow, and some initials on her hip.

As we got her settled on the bed, I covered her again and finally looked at her face. At her. At the very old, edentulous, but pretty woman, obviously who'd had a defiant spirit, who had tattooed herself, and who loved, perhaps recklessly, enough to tell the world.

I never made that mistake again. I never let my needs and feelings supersede trying to find out who my patient was or had been.

And I took that experience to heart. A few weeks later my friend, Freida, and I went to Yakima, the nearest city with a reputable tattoo parlor, and we got tattoos. Mine is beautiful and more than thirty years old now.

I've never regretted the fact that I've got a permanent reminder to others that I'm more than my tattered old body would have them believe. I hope they'll see that at one time I'd been a hopeful woman. I hope they will try to imagine who I might have been. I hope it will stir their heart too.

. . . .

HOT DOG BOY'S DAY, AUGUST 15, 1969

By Jerry Keelen

Woodstock. I well remember not being there. Our FM transistor radios, tuned to WNEW 102.7, the coolest station, told us that not far north, up in New York State, a sizable part of humanity in the full bloom of youth was surging toward the epicenter of the hip world to be part of the coolest, purest, greatest, mind-bending music event in history.

Bubby and I listened wistfully. "We should go." Bubby said. "Bands, dope, millions of girls, plus alcohol. No one checking."

"How?" I asked petulantly. "You don't even drive and my mom would kill me even at the suggestion that we take her car." At that point I had a new driver's license, but the car aside, Mom would say "No," and make life miserable for the rest of the summer for the audacity of asking.

"You got here early?" Bubby asked.

"Yeah, Bob wanted me in early to help open up." It was Friday of a hot week in mid-August and we could see Bob Pasciewicz, our boss at Seaside Baths, a boardwalk fast food and locker concession, down by the road waving cars into the parking lot.

"I hate that guy," Bubby said with his usual patrician distain. That's the way Bubby was. Dirty blonde hair, green eyes, a little pudgy and a long nose to look down. He claimed with contrarian pride to be a descendent of Aaron Burr. He'd say things like "My family is Episcopalian. That's the best religion. You don't have to go to church, but when you do they give you wine."

Seaside Baths, Seaside Heights, NJ

I liked, maybe more accurately tolerated, Bubs as a summertime friend, but I stopped hanging out with him at night after he almost got me killed twice. The first time by running his bicycle in front of a speeding motorcycle on Route 35 causing a crash that amazingly caused us no harm from either the out-of-control motorcycle or any of the resulting flying bike parts. The motorcycle guy was big and angry and when he got up from the curb said we were dead, but we outran him. The next time we dragged my eight- foot pram to the beach for an after dark paddle. I pushed Bubs out through the little waves and he started flailing with the oars and ended up about 50 yards out and I was yelling at him to come back to shore and get me. "I don't know how to row," he said. "Throw out the anchor, you moron," I yelled back. He did, but not before the boat had drifted another hundred yards away. I can swim, but I'm no champ and night swimming in the ocean is stupid, as the fisherman over at the Casino Pier will attest having hooked many hammerhead sharks foraging the area in the warm summer waters. I made it and Bubby helped pull me over the gunnel. I rowed us back to shore and I told Bubby that was it for us.

"Bob's not so bad."

"That's because he likes you." Bubby was correct, Bob liked me because I worked a lot of hours and cared enough to do a good job, and showed up every time and on time, and didn't eat too much or give away ice cream cups or frozen Snickers bars to my friends and a few more things I'll get to later. Bob also said there would be a bonus for me, and only me, at the end of the season and it was shaping up to be a great season with no rained-out weekends and a strange pattern of rainy nights and sunny days. Hot too. Real fine beach weather. Bob said it was his best year in ten since he started running the Seaside Baths parking lot, food concession and changing rooms.

"Look, I've got to get the grille going and get the old hot dogs out, Bubby. You think you can pour syrup into the soda machines?"

"Right, boss. You're another Bob."

"I'm not your boss. I wonder who's going to show up today anyway."

The first part of the answer came walking in. It was Paul, a shortish, skinny kid, recently hired. Paul was from Pennsylvania. He always wore the same faded red T-shirt and blue jeans. Nice, but a slow learner with a voracious appetite. When Paul started about ten days back, he fell victim to Tommy's pirate attack. Tommy is Bob's seven-year-old son who talks like a pirate and feels entitled to "run one through" the counter boys which meant that he would sneak up from behind and give a running karate chop to his victim's back. A surprise blow like that, even from a smallish boy, was painful and spine jarring. I know because he got me on my first day early in the summer. Since then, I and the other counter boys (he didn't attack the two counter girls for some reason) were wary of Tommy and developed a kind of sixth sense about his whereabouts. But he got Paul good. Paul was ready to quit. We promised him all the Sealtest ice cream cups he could eat. He stayed. Terry, Bob's wife and Tommy's prescription sunglasses wearing mother, sat on her padded stool by the bath house entrance, at the ready to comfort Tommy after Bob's latest scolding.

"Hey Paul, glad you're here. You want to grab yesterday's left-over dogs and a box of new ones from the freezer? You could also make sure the ketchup and mustard bottles are filled up and stick some popsicle sticks in about 20 Snickers bars and throw them in the small freezer."

Some of my friends worked further down the boardwalk for concession owners who practiced sharp business practices and who were notoriously cheap. Bob wasn't like that but he had his ways, one of which was to re-heat and sell yesterday's leftover shriveled dogs. If you rolled them on the hot grille they'd plump and other than being darker brown, they might pass the untrained eye as fresh. The problem was that the casing would thicken and toughen, be hard to bite and chew, and when the dog cooled it would look like a thickly furrowed beef jerky. A few people asked for twice-cooked hot dogs, but most were not pleased with them.

Seaside Heights Beach and Boardwalk circa 1969

I'd assess the buyers to predict which ones likely would keck and demand their money back. If anyone asked, I'd honestly reply, "You might want to wait ten minutes." If Bob wasn't around, I'd tell them to dump the dog in the trash and give them a new one. The moral I took from this is to never be the first customers served in the morning at a food concession stand.

The greasy dogs began to sizzle and smell tasty. Just another sound and flavor adding to the mélange of ocean, beach and boardwalk sounds and smells of pizza, sausage and peppers, sun tan lotion, and salt air.

The boardwalk loudspeaker system blurted out a yelp of ear-piercing feedback followed by, "Testing, testing, one, two, three, four," as it did every morning. It was loud. It had to be, because it was in competition with the ocean, birds, the beachgoers yacking and radios, and the carnival sounds emanating from the food stands, barkers, wheels of chance, pin-ball machines, the merry-go-round pavilions, pier rides and the usually present ocean breeze. We'd be hearing plenty more from the life guard central sound system during the course of the day.

WNEW said that the Woodstock promoters were telling people to stay way. That only raised our envy and desire to go. We heard that Richie Haven's would be the first act, his wild guitar strumming sure to rouse the concert goers.

A local girl, Jody, punched in for work about 9:30. There were two kinds of kids who worked at Seaside Baths, locals who lived in Seaside year-round and went by bus to Central Regional High School on the mainland, they all knew each other, and summer visitors from North Jersey and the Philadelphia area. Bubby and I were among the latter, whose parents had summer homes in the little towns close by Seaside Heights.

Jody had a twin brother whom we knew, but who worked someplace else on the boardwalk. She was good natured and a willing worker (unusual for the locals), but had trouble calculating prices and change. In those days the cash register didn't do anything except open and close and hand calculators were yet to make it to the masses. A typical family order might be 7 dogs at 75 cents each, four sodas at 35 cents each, three frozen Snickers bars at 8 cents each and a couple of bags of chips at 10 cents each. Me and Bubby and two other guys, cousins Burt and George, from the visitor class, after a few hundred customers could do the addition in our heads. On the bigger orders Jody and the other locals would place the order on the counter and look at one of us, usually me, and we'd say, for example, "$7.09". There was no sales tax back then to complicate things. A few people would look baffled or angry and say "Wait a minute that can't be right, he did that in his head." But it almost always was accurate.

The whistles of the lifeguards rising above the beach noise were more often and more piercingly urgent than usual. "Swimming is permitted only between the red flags in front of the lifeguard stands," the loudspeaker blared.

Bob's parking lot was almost filled and he was directing latecomers' cars into the remaining crannies. Terry was collecting money for our green and yellow rental beach umbrellas and inflatable rafts. Families were changing into their swimsuits in the locker rooms, teen boys with Lodi High School Wrestling shirts were doing pushups to pump up some muscles before their shirtless debut. Girls, I suspected, worked on their makeup, hair and bikinis. The beach was crowded and the day trippers were beginning to get hungry. The smell of grilled hot dogs drifted over the scene. The crowd around our concession counter began to grow.

Cousins Burt and George showed up just in time. Paul had eaten two Sealtest chocolate ice cream cups and two hot dogs and was sidling up to mooch another dog.

Don Jennings, a local showed up too. Don was a 16-year-old, big shouldered baby-blue-eyed adonis surfer stud, and he knew it. He wasn't interested in working hard, or at all if he could help it. He would pour sodas from the soda machines, Coke, Orange and Fresca, but his main function seemed to be to gaze out onto the beach scene and look mysterious and dreamy-eyed. But there was a steady flow of girls from Central Regional wanting nothing more than to buy a soda from Don. Older women seemed to favor Don's line too. "Did you see those eyes?" was common refrain. Don also had a cadre of surfing buddies who rolled out of bed late in the morning hungry. Guys like Squirrel O'Riley, possibly the best surfer, or at least the craziest daredevil one, in the area would come around and Don would sneak him free food. Bob knew this, but on balance Don was good for business when he deigned to show up.

"Woodstock is an out-of-control people's festival. The promoters have given up collecting tickets and Max Yasgur's farm has been overrun by partying music fans," WNEW said. A life altering time up in New York and we were stuck in Seaside Heights dutifully serving a vastly different crowd.

Burt found a praying mantis somewhere by the freezer and put it into a two-gallon empty pickle relish jar. It was one of the big straw-brown colored ones and seemed at home in the jar despite the pickle smell. Maybe mantis can't smell. "Put it up on the high shelf above the chips," I said thinking that I heard somewhere that it was illegal to kill a praying mantis and not wanting gross out the customers too much.

A Seaside Heights police cruiser pulled up through the parking lot. Two cops got out, walked up the ramp to the boardwalk and waited by the beach pass hand stamper's kiosk. The cops I knew usually came around about 4 o'clock for a hot dog and soda snack. They would ritually offer to pay, and I would ritually refuse their money saying that Bob would fire me if I let them pay. That way they felt like they were doing me a favor. Bob ran a cash business and appreciated as much police presence as he could get. He knew if he needed them, they would be there and be very helpful. But these cops at the kiosk were bruisers, auxiliaries hired by Seaside Heights for the season to assist with crowd control and manhandle the occasional out of control drunk.

The present mission of these auxiliaries soon became apparent. Two lifeguards each with a hand cinched around an arm were escorting an angry bedraggled, shirtless, paunchy middle-aged man up from the beach. I recognized the phenomenon of the man saved from drowning who claimed that he was an excellent swimmer who didn't need saving because he was in no danger and the lifeguards overstepped and that they needed to back off, which for added emphasis he threw a couple of punches. In those days the guards were itinerant pros hired for water duties, but also for crowd control. The kind of guys paid by the pound.

"Officer, he's all yours. He took a swing at me and another at Ricky. You let us know if you want us to sign to file charges." At this point the man's wife, dragging blankets and beach chairs had caught up and began yelling, "He didn't do anything. Take your hands off him. I'm going to re..." The officer cut her off, saying, "You this guy's wife? Meet us down at the police station on Sherman Avenue in about an hour. We'll let you know if Mister is going before the judge today or tomorrow morning." Mister was drained at this point and submissively got in the back of the cruiser. This was a scene that happened every so often, when a guy was embarrassed about being saved. It's inexplicable, but probably has something to do with a wounded male ego. I asked my regular cops what happens to people like that. They said that after an hour sitting in the temporary lock-up they come to their senses apologize for being a jerk, get the evil eye from their wife and then get sent home without charges.

Pauly did get that third, maybe fourth, hot dog and now is standing in front of me saying with earnestness, "I feel sick. I need to go home." I said, "What kind of sick?" "Stomach. It's killing me." "I wonder why? Don't forget to punch out." Well, Paul was a net loss that day, but Bob didn't fuss too much about employes' food consumption. He knew that teenagers need to eat and the free food perk was a way to attract low wage workers who were always in short supply on the boardwalk.

"Attention, lost child alert," the loudspeaker blared. "Anyone looking for Ronald, about 4, red hair, blue shirt please go to the Dupont Street beach entrance." Lots of kids got lost every day. The beach is a confusing place once you wander into the crowd even a few dozen feet from your blanket. Kids did this all the time while their guardians fell asleep or got engrossed in their page-turner beach read. Then they wander farther away.

Usually, they cry and some kind hearted adult will bring them to the nearest boardwalk attendant. As far as I know no kid ever stayed lost.

The crowd around the counter was growing and we were throwing hot dogs on the grille fast, filling soda orders and selling ice cream non-stop. Now Kimmie was here piling up an order and looking for a price. “$12.24,” George yelled. I mentally double checked. He got it right. Kimmie was another Central Regional kid, kind of chunky with lots of makeup, who mostly showed up when tipped-off that Don Jennings was there. Don never acknowledged Kim’s existence as far as we could tell. But she was a hard enough worker and the rest of us were glad to have her around.

Burt was trying to catch a big fly off the counter with his hand. He was quick and already caught one to feed to Deano the praying mantis. Deano was even quicker, catching the gift fly in the gripper hands at the end of it long arms. Mantis eat their flies alive holding head and tail respectively in each in each hand and spinning it like a corn on the cob until the fly is fully eaten. This new fly was taunting Burt, flying off at the last instant eluding the swoop of his hand. Just then out of the corner of my eye I saw the attack coming. Burt’s attention was totally locked in on the fly and he was oblivious to the approaching danger. The Max Baer Day Campers field trip to the beach had landed at Seaside Baths and a few of the kids were buzzing around the food counter while their counselors smoked over by boardwalk fence. I yelled to Burt, but it was too late. Two campers about 10 or 11 years old grabbed the squeezable ketchup and mustard dispensers from the counter and began firing away at Burt. Our dispensers were super flexible and wide gauged – weapons grade condiment shooters. This sort of thing happened about once a week, so we were not unaware of the threat. These kids were good and they picked their mark well. I left the grille and went over and got the counselors. They shrugged and apologized, apparently all in a day’s work for them, and the

Max Baer campers went away, no doubt telling tales of bagging a big one. We got Burt one of Bob's spare T-shirts from Terry and life went on.

WNEW said, traffic was backed up for miles on soggy hardly passable rural New York farm country roads. The festival site was already a mud pit owing to days of rain the week before. Bands were having trouble getting there. There were rumblings of poor sanitation, lack of water and food and bad drugs. Bubby, Burt, George and I were the only Seaside Baths employes who knew or cared. Our envy of missing out on the festival of festivals was fading with each news update.

A middle-aged woman in a green sequined swimsuit came by. She was sweating and grouchy. "Gimme a Freshka," she said with her classic Staten Island accent. Bubs our resident patrician laughed. "We don't have FreshKa. You mean Fresca?" "Don't get wise with me kid, you know what I want." I jumped in, "Yes ma'am, medium or large?" "Big one." I pushed the Fresca button on the soda machine and drained her a large one. "Here you are. That will be 35 cents please ma'am. Would you like anything else?" Green sequined woman looked at the Fresca sitting there on the counter in a paper cup and said, "It's warm. I don't want it." I said as she was turning away. "How do you know? You haven't even touched it." Bubs was laughing at me. She turned away and was gone. In fact, she was correct. The soda machines in those days spewed out a mix of flavored syrups and carbonated water from a cannister under the counter. The refrigerant coils after a while cannot keep pace with the volume of liquid flowing into paper cups and the soda, if not warm, is not very cold either. Most people can live with the fiction that they are getting a coolish drink, because they are feeling a vacation kind of bon homme and Seaside Baths is obviously not the Ritz.

The afternoon was setting in and business was quieting down. There is a wonderful blend of rising afternoon wind, waves, guard whistles, laughing gulls "Haw, Haw, Hawing", bells and sirens from the pier rides that, if you stop and take it in, is audio-hypnotic. That's when "Ritchie" showed up. We knew he was "Ritchie" because that's what the it said on the gold chain around his hairy tanned neck. Ritchie said, "Gentlemen, I'll have two of your finest hot dogs, two Coca-Colas and two packs of onion chips. By the way, let me introduce you to Ursala." Ursala was a six-foot, blonde beauty, probably middle age plus a few years. She was wearing white bikini and looked amazing even to us young fellows. "Boys, Ursala's a movie star in Sweden." I asked Ritchie if any of her movies were shown in America. He said not likely, she makes art house movies. I had no idea what an "art house" movie was, but she sure was built to impress. We gave Ritchie our

finest dogs and drinks. He generously thanked us and put a $10 bill on the counter and said "Keep the change." It was the first time all summer that anyone offered a tip. Burt said "Ritchie's the man." We, at least the boys, all agreed.

"Blat", the boardwalk loud speaker roared back to life. There had been several more lost boys since Ronald. No girls for some reason. Girls rarely get lost it seems. The Friday night fireworks were touted a couple of times, but all in all a slow day at the central guard pavilion. Until now. "You, there by the Sheridan Avenue entrance in the red trunks." We knew by the indignant tone what was coming. "Go easy on that girl, this is a family beach. You know who I'm talking about, yes, you! Stop it now or the guards will remove you two from the beach."

That one happened maybe every other day and was always a crowd pleaser.

There were some regulars that didn't really have anything to do with Seaside Baths. I mentioned Squirrel O'Riley. He was small and muscular like a gymnast and had a pleasing face that looked like the human version of a chipmunk. He was best friends with Don Jennings and charming enough that no one objected when he came behind the counter to help himself to snacks and serve customers like the rest of us, but for free. Squirrel was the crazy man who surfed between the pilings of the Casino Pier and took off on huge shore break waves that would without doubt pile drive any normal surfer into the sand causing devastating injury or death. Squirrel apparently didn't have a death-wish, he was just quick enough to flip out over the back of the wave before it went Kaboom and paddle out to his amazed friends to catch the next one.

Another regular was Diane, a girl with straight long blonde hair and a look something like the California girl ideal of the day. Diane would come around looking for Don or Squirrel or some of their surfer friends to see what beach they'd be surfing that evening. She showed up too late. Don was long gone. I was surprised that she came over by the grille which was more or less my permanent station and asked, "Where are you surfing tonight?" I wasn't in the same league with the locals, but I did surf often and in fact coincidentally had surfed with Diane a couple of times. She mostly floated around beyond the break and talked to the surfer boys. I don't recall what we talked about or ever seeing her catch a wave. Looking back, I see that she had discovered the perfect a way to meet boys. She was nice. I told Diane the plain disappointing truth, "By the time I'm done closing up here it will be 6 o'clock. The sun's going down so early now I won't get home in time to get the board and hit the waves until it's almost dark. I've developed a thing about being in the water when it's dark. Sorry to say. I hope you catch some good ones."

Diane left with a sigh.

The two regular cops showed up with Bob. "Afternoon officers," I said. "The usual?"

"Yep."

"Coming up. Say Bob did you see that Ritchie guy in the lot?"

"The guy with the tall blonde?"

“Right. He says she’s a big star in Sweden. Some type of art house movies.”

The cops laughed. “’Art house’, that’s a good one. What he meant was she’s a porn star.”

“Oh. He seems like a nice guy.”

“He probably is. Lots of money in that business. We’re keeping an eye on him. Drives a big Lincoln, New York plates, right Bob?”

“Yeah, took up two parking spaces.”

“A good day today,” Bob said pointing in the direction of the vault. “There are a few umbrellas left on the beach. Give me a hand we’ll round them up and get this place cleaned up and shut down.”

“Okay,” I said. Getting the stuff off the beach would kill any chance of getting out early. After that I’d do my OCD cleaning of the grille, a process that took a good 20 minutes.

It’s after five. Richie Havens was on stage at Woodstock. I’m putting elbow grease into getting the hot dog scorched carbon off the grille surface. I always started with vegetable oil and a large coiled steel scrubber which is basically a commercial grade Brillo pad. Tommy sidles up while I’m rhythmically scrubbing up and down. Tommy shows me the drawings he did today. We had a reproachment after the surprise pirate attack. I showed him how to draw a pirate, and then a pirate ship and then flowers for his mom and he like drawing and seemed to have some talent. I told him about Mr. Pugh and the black spot from *Treasure Island* and when he seemed interested, I got him a kid’s version of the book with pictures. I moved on to the grinding stone phase, which is what makes the solid iron top of the grille look silvery new again.

Bob came in and dropped near exhausted on a wooden stool. He said, “I really like the way that grille looks. I’ve never had anyone do that good of a job.”

I said, “There’s probably something wrong with me. I love to see the old grille shine.”

Then he said, “No one’s ever gotten through to Tommy either. You seem to be able to calm him down.”

“He’s a good kid. You might read him a book at night sometimes. That worked for me when I was little.” I handed him *Treasure Island*, put the grinding stone in its cubby, said goodnight to Tommy and Bob and went home.

Woodstock was a personal experience I did not get to have. I didn’t realize it at the time, but being a hot dog boy at the Jersey Shore was quite a remarkable life forming experience too. Maybe even a more lasting and meaningful one than a muddy music festival.

It was 6 pm. and Richie Havens was finishing the first of his seven heroic sets that August night in New York, keeping the massive and still gathering crowd mollified while the other acts made their way to the show.

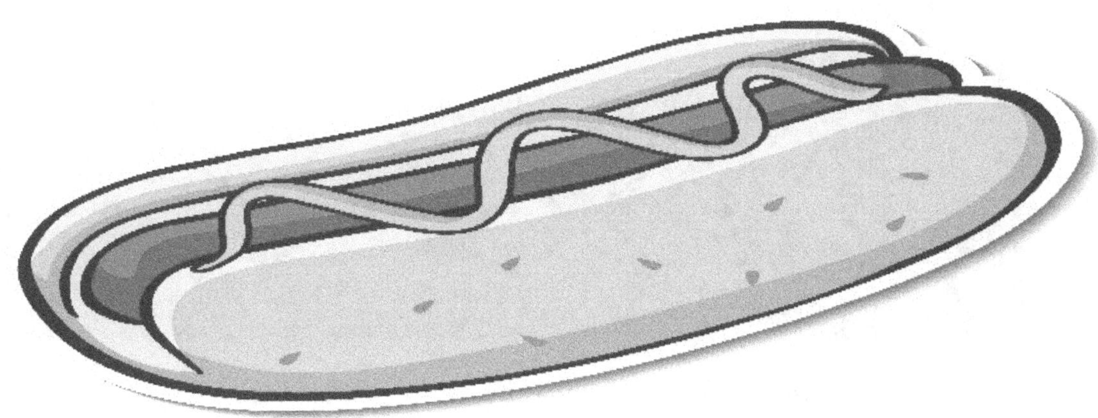

Part Four, Heard on the trail

Tucson Mountain Park Wash near the end of the trail home. Santa Catalina Mountains in background

+ It's easy to get lost if you have misidentified your destination. NJ

+THE GYM ROWER

I, rowing a machine, landlocked in a desert gym, am transported in my mind 2,500 miles away to the Navesink estuary, a tidal arm of the Atlantic Ocean I have often rowed and know well. I imagine snapper blues jumping, osprey above, herring and great black back gulls on channel markers, the smell of salty spray and seaweed, diamond back terrapins poking up to breathe and look. There is a certain point where the steady flow of the river stops and the swells of the deeper, wider water pushed by the Atlantic tide lifts the boat and caresses the oars. It's then that I know I'm experiencing a power of nature far beyond my circumspect little world. JK

+But what is life without many misunderstandings and their humor as well as the opportunity to improve our understanding of each other? NJ

+Men and Women are stupid, but in different ways, and therein lies the fate of the species. JK

+Don't recreate the wheel, find the artisan! NJ

+I'm reminded that the best thing I've learned at this stage of life is to smile, nod approvingly when I can, smile, and butt out. NJ

Walking the sandbars of Barnegat Bay, New Jersey in search of clams.
What could possibly go wrong?

Snow-capped Santa Catalinas. Photo taken from Painted Hills Trail, Tucson

SmartSign.com • 800-952-1457 • K2-1130

www.ingramcontent.com/pod-product-compliance
Lightning Source LLC
LaVergne TN
LVHW061255100826
845148LV00008B/1127
9781637951712